to Jackson, Madison, and Samantha
— DHA

to Faye — JB

Published in the United States in 2004 by Handprint Books
413 Sixth Avenue
Brooklyn, New York 11215
www.handprintbooks.com

Book design by April Ward

First Edition
Printed in China
ISBN: 1-59354-050-7
2 4 6 8 10 9 7 5 3 1

BLESS THIS MOUSE

By DIANNA HUTTS ASTON   Illustrated by JOHN BUTLER

Handprint Books Brooklyn, New York

In the morning-time woods
    where night creatures play,
Sits a sleepy-eyed mouse, with prayers to say,
    A sleepy-eyed mouse, quite small and gray—
Ready to dream the day away.

Bless Fawn, Raccoon,

Skunk, and Snail.

Bless stripes and rings and spots and trails.

Bless Bear and Possum,
Wolf and Owl.

Bless fur and tails
and hoots and howls.

Bless the pokers,
and the peepers.

Bless the fliers,
and the leapers.

Bless all creatures North and South.

Bless trees,

and trunks,

and roots,

and boughs.

Bless all creatures
East and West.

Bless Mama, bless Papa—
I love them best.

Bless the white of the moon,
the black on the berry,

The gold of the sun,
the red on the cherry.

Bless the cap on the nut,
the web and the dew.

Bless the leaves

and the seeds...

Bless this mouse, too.

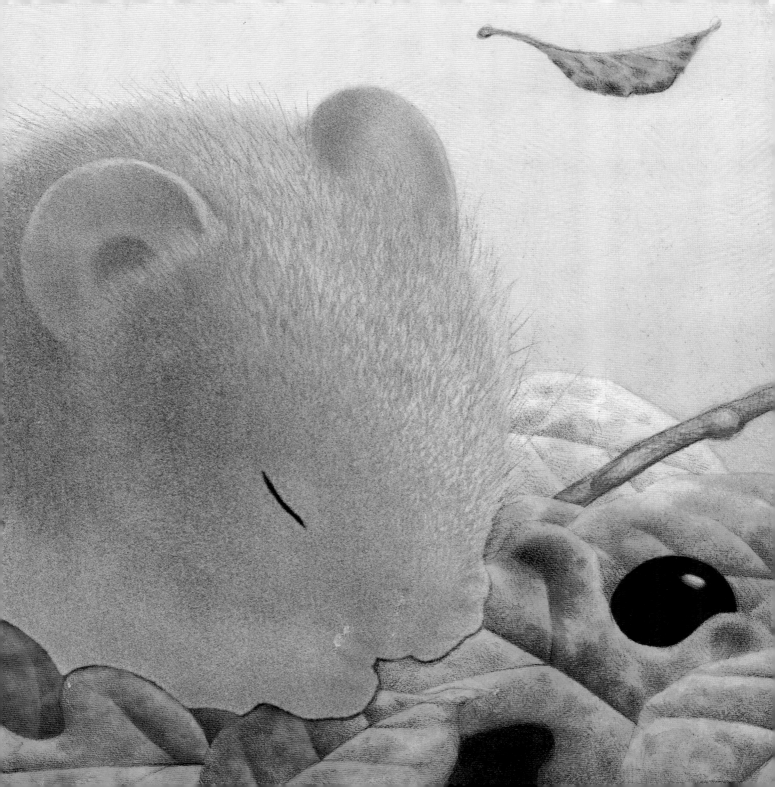